# The KALEIDOSCOPE PONY

BY

# AINSLIE SHERIDAN

FOX KIT PRESS
WWW.FOXKITPRESS.COM

*For my wonderful daughter Marleny*

**THE KALEIDOSCOPE PONY**
**Written & Illustrated by Ainslie Sheridan**

First Edition, First Printing
Published by
FOX KIT PRESS
14 Breezy Point Road, Acton, MA 01720
www.foxkitpress.com

Cover and book design by Arrow Graphics, Inc.
info@arrow1.com
Printed in China

ISBN-13:  978-0-9785124-0-8
ISBN-10:  0-9785124-0-5
Library of Congress Control Number: 2006906058

*And now here is my secret, a very simple secret:*
*It is only with the heart that one can see rightly;*
*what is essential is invisible to the eye.*

—The Fox in *The Little Prince*,
Antoine de Saint-Exupéry

*I have heard of reasons manifold*
*Why love must needs be blind,*
*But this the best of all I hold—*
*His eyes are in his mind.*

*What outward form and feature are*
*He guesseth but in part;*
*But what within is good and fair*
*He seeth with the heart.*

—Samuel Taylor Coleridge

# Acknowledgements

I would like to thank Lily, Emma, and Stephen Crockett, Cherry Brewster, Cindy Powell, Henry Vaillant, M.D., and Alec Engell for portraying the characters in this book. I would also like to thank C. Bennett Scopes for supplying the "normal" kaleidoscopic images as well as Hayley's golden kaleidoscope. Thank you to Samii Clothes for providing the magical attire. I am also grateful to Emerson Hospital for the use of one of their rooms for the hospital scenes. Many thanks to Tricia O'Connor for giving me the real Kip. And, last but not least, a special thanks to Kip herself, who lives with me in Acton, Massachusetts, and who continues to enchant all those who come to know her.

hello! My name is Hayley Fletcher. I want to tell you about something special. It all began one day in March, just after Mom and I moved to Concord, Massachusetts. I didn't want to leave San Jose. All my friends were in California and so was my Dad. He's an engineer and had to finish a project. He would visit Mom and me, but we wouldn't live together as a family for months and months. I went from a nice home with orange trees and rosebushes to an old colonial house with cold drafts and a yard full of snow and mud. Anyway, as my Dad says, that's just background. What I really want to tell you is the most important and exciting adventure of my life.

The day after we moved, I was sitting in the kitchen watching big flakes of wet snow falling in the field when, off in the distance, I saw what looked like a small pony. But I wasn't sure. So I threw on my parka, pulled on my boots, and raced out the back door to the fence line that separates our yard from the field. It *was* a pony! She was so skinny I could see every rib. Her brown and white coat looked dull and matted with dirt. Her body was miserable but her eyes were beautiful—soft and gentle.

"Wait here, girl, I'll be right back," I said. In the house I grabbed a bag of carrots and an apple, and then I ran back. She was still there.

It was as if she understood! The air filled with the sound of sweet crunching. Then I gave her carrots.

"Don't worry, girl," I said, stroking her soft neck. "I'll come back with something for you to eat every day. You won't go hungry anymore."

Every day I fed the pony after school. She was either waiting at the fence or came trotting up as soon as she saw me. And because she was happy, I was happy, too.

But just when the pony's ribs were beginning to disappear, I had a bad accident. Mom wasn't home and I didn't have anything to do. So I turned on the gas oven and began what I thought would be a great science experiment. I don't remember anything now except burning fire in my face. I woke up later somewhere else and couldn't see. I went to touch my eyes but a hand closed over mine. I smelled a familiar woodsy scent.

"Dad!"

"I'm right here, Sweetheart. As soon as Mom called I took the next flight to Boston."

"I'm here, too, Hayley," said Mom.

My eyes burned and itched, like someone had thrown sand—a ton of sand—into them. I got scared. "My eyes hurt!" I yelled. "Where am I?"

"Hayley, I'm Dr. Noble. You're in the hospital. I know your eyes hurt but they'll be as good as new. The bandage will come off in a week. And then you can go home."

"A week? I won't be able to see for a whole week?" I suddenly remembered my friend in the field. "And the pony, who will take care of her?"

"The pony is fine. I know this sounds incredible," Mom said, "but this morning when I drove home to pick up some of your things, I saw a woman giving her hay."

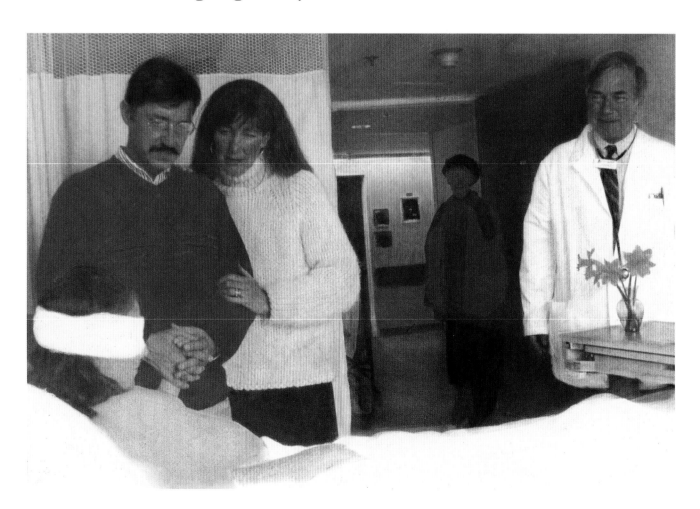

That night Mom slept in the hospital bed next to mine.
I listened to her steady breathing and wondered if what she said was true. I'd never seen anyone around the field, much less near the pony. Why would somebody appear out of nowhere just when I couldn't be there? And where had this lady been when the pony really needed her? I decided Mom had told me a white lie. She didn't want me to worry. But it wasn't a white lie to me. I needed to know if the pony had food, and I didn't care if it made me worry.

Even though the nurse had given me pain medicine, my eyes still stung so badly that I couldn't sleep. I tossed and turned. I felt a cold draft on my neck. A window near my bed must have been open. I wished the pony had wings like the Greek horse Pegasus. She'd fly to the window and I'd hop on her back. A moonlit night and a field of stars would light our way home.

"Your mother is right. The pony is fine."

I awoke with a start to a strange voice. "Who are you?"

"A volunteer."

Volunteers brought me my meals, but her voice sounded different, as if she came from far away and long ago.

"A volunteer here at the hospital?" I asked.

She ignored my question. "I've brought you a present. When your bandage comes off, look into it. You'll see that Kip is fine."

"Kip," I repeated.

"That's her name. When it comes time, look into this and you'll see what you need to know."

I felt a long cylinder wrapped in paper. There were ribbons, too. "But what is this and who—"

"Each time you look—and this is very important—you must remember that one truly sees with the heart."

The door clicked shut and she was gone. I heard Mom's steady breathing. She was still asleep.

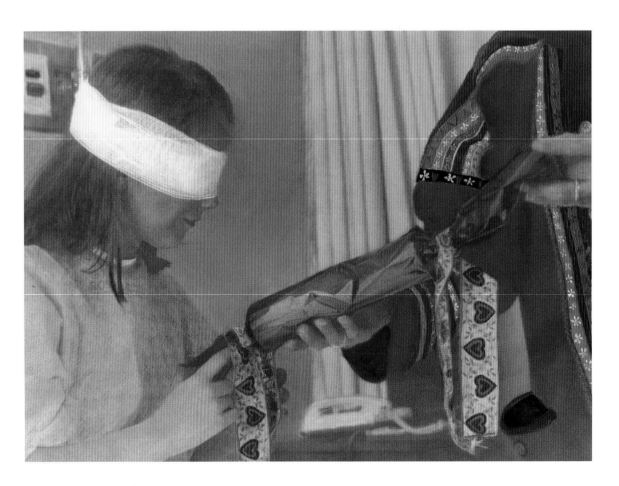

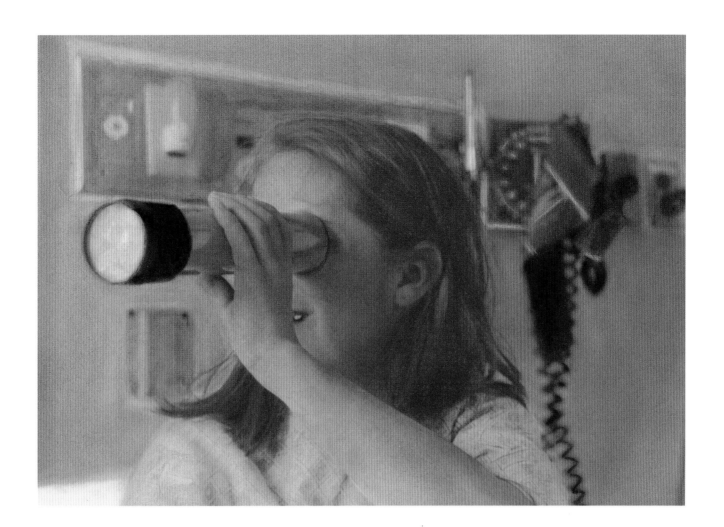

Finally, after five long days, Dr. Noble came to take my bandage off. I was happy but scared, too. I took a deep breath as I felt the gauze unwinding. Suddenly, a blast of yellow-white light! I squinted and blinked. And there was Mom. She looked so beautiful. Then I saw it— wrapped in shiny purple paper and tied with a ribbon with red hearts. It was the present from the strange woman.

"We still don't know who she is," said Mom. It bothered her that she had slept when a stranger had come in. "But I'm sure she must work at the hospital."

I picked up the gift. The paper and ribbon just slid right off and fell to the floor. I hadn't even tried to unwrap it. And there in my hands was a beautiful gold cylinder. It was a kaleidoscope.

"Remember, one truly sees with the heart." The woman's words came into my head as if she were right there whispering in my ear. I held the kaleidoscope up to my eye and gasped.

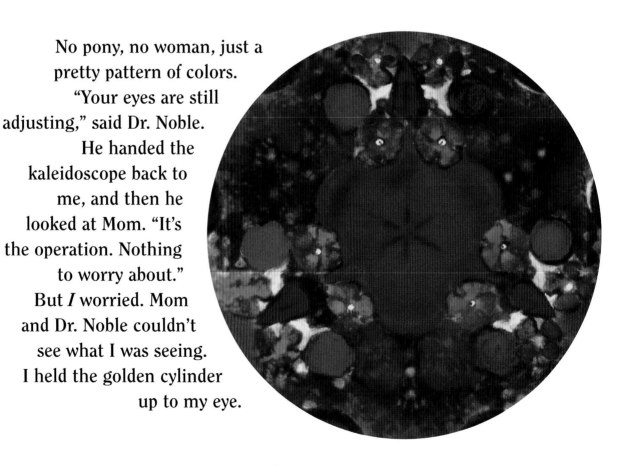

It was the pony—Kip—wearing
a beautiful halter, and a
woman dressed in a
gorgeous winter coat!
They looked like they
were in a fairy tale.
"Mom, look! It's
Kip and a woman."
Mom held the
kaleidoscope to her
eye, but when she put
it down I could tell that
she hadn't seen what I
had seen. She glanced at
Dr. Noble and handed him the
kaleidoscope. He looked through
it and described what he saw.

No pony, no woman, just a
pretty pattern of colors.
"Your eyes are still
adjusting," said Dr. Noble.
He handed the
kaleidoscope back to
me, and then he
looked at Mom. "It's
the operation. Nothing
to worry about."
But *I* worried. Mom
and Dr. Noble couldn't
see what I was seeing.
I held the golden cylinder
up to my eye.

Again, Kip and the woman, but this time a different image! They were looking right at me and the woman was waving.

"See with your heart, not with your eyes." The woman's voice sounded in my head.

"I know why you and Dr. Noble can't see what I see!" I exclaimed.

"Why, Hayley?" Mom asked.

"Because you don't love the pony the way I do." Mom looked at Dr. Noble and then stroked my cheek with her hand.

"That must be the reason," she said.

"It's the best one I can think of," said Dr. Noble.

But I wasn't trying to think up the "best" reason! Mom and Dr. Noble couldn't see what I was seeing because they were looking only with their eyes. I wondered why adults sometimes said that they believed what children said when they didn't believe it—not at all.

When I got home I wasn't allowed to go outside for ten days because Dr. Noble said I could get an infection. So I spent hours looking out the window for Kip, but didn't see her—not ever. I was afraid she was gone or hurt. Mom said she hadn't seen her either. I had a hard time sleeping and could barely eat. Late one afternoon while Mom was running errands, I put on my jacket and went out to look for Kip. It had snowed the night before so I didn't think there would be any dirt to get in my eyes. I climbed over the fence and walked through the drifts of snow. The wind howled, my eyes stung, and it hurt to take a breath.

With each step I felt more and more scared. Mom had warned me never to walk across the field. It was private property, she said, and we didn't know if the pony was trained. She worried that Kip might accidentally kick me. I turned and looked back at my house. The light in the windows seemed far away. But I kept on going. The wind was roaring even more loudly.

I came to the end of the field but still I couldn't see Kip. Several trails led to the forest. I didn't know which one to take. I was afraid I'd get lost. My face felt frozen and I couldn't feel my fingers or toes. I was about to turn back when I saw something red glittering on a pine tree. I looked closer. It was an image of the flying Greek horse Pegasus. An arrow pointed down one path that ran behind a stand of pines. I knew I was meant to go that way.

As soon as I entered the woods the wind stopped completely. The only sound I heard was my feet crunching through a top layer of thin ice that had formed over the deep snow. I crossed a small footbridge. The frozen stream sparkled below like a sheet of diamonds. The moon came out and seemed to grow brighter with each step I took. The air felt warmer, then warmer still. I could feel my fingers and toes again.

I walked through a grove of birch trees and came to a rickety old gate. Then I heard it—a small whinny! I tried to peer over the gate but it was too tall. So I climbed up halfway. There was Kip. And there was the woman in the kaleidoscope!

They both looked like they stepped out of a fairy tale. My heart beat so loudly that I was sure she could hear it. I couldn't catch my breath. Questions raced through my head. How did she…? Why was she…? Who was she?

Suddenly, my foot slipped on the gate and made a loud noise. Kip and the woman turned and looked straight at me. I jumped down and started to run away as fast as I could.

"Hayley! Wait!" the woman called.

But she wasn't yelling. Her voice sounded inside my head—softly, firmly—like the voice in the hospital. I turned and looked back. The gate swung gently open. Kip and the woman still stood exactly where I had seen them.

"We've been expecting you," she said. Now smiling, she held up a welcoming hand. "Come in. Come visit with us."

I recognized that voice. She had given me the kaleidoscope! I started through the gate that seemed to have opened by itself. Then another incredible thing happened.

My own jacket was gone and I was dressed like the woman—in magical winter clothing—hat, mittens, and coat!

"You gave me the kaleidoscope," I said.

"Your mother told you that Kip was fine. The kaleidoscope told you that, too, in another way. But you needed to see for yourself. You may stay only a little while. Come, there's time enough for one ride."

As the woman led Kip and me through the forest, the stars twinkled and the moon was so bright that I felt I was between night and day. The warmth of Kip's body made me warm. I felt happy and safe. I couldn't imagine being anywhere else.

But then the woman came to a stop.

"You must go home now. Listen to your mother and take care of those eyes so they heal."

"And my heart?" I asked, remembering what she had told me in the hospital. I was sure my heart would break if I couldn't see Kip again.

"Taking care of one's heart never stops."

"Will I see Kip again?"

"See with your heart and you will." Her face told me our visit was over. As soon as I turned and stepped back through the gate, the magical winter clothing disappeared. Once again I was dressed in my dark blue parka and ski band. But I didn't feel cold. As I walked through the drifts of snow, a golden moon and a field of stars lit my way home.

My eyes healed, but Kip was gone. As time passed I even began to wonder if I had imagined the magical time in the woods, or had dreamt it. And I never saw Kip—or the woman—in the kaleidoscope again. I looked through it every day when I got home from school, and the first thing in the morning on weekends. I saw designs like Mom and Dr. Noble described that day in the hospital. Each one beautiful and unique, but just designs.

I wasn't as lonely as before. I made some friends and even had a sleepover. Mom bought pizza and we rented a Disney movie. We had a lot of fun, eating, talking, and just being silly. But before I went to sleep I checked the images in the kaleidoscope. I let the other girls look, too, because I wanted to know if they were seeing what I saw. They were: just pretty patterns.

My ninth birthday fell on a Friday in May. Dad was still in California, and I felt lonely for the first time in ages. I asked Mom if I could stay home with her. But Mom said no, that I'd missed too much school already because of my accident. I had fun at school, though. We learned how sailors navigate the seas by looking at the stars and how they predict the weather by the color of the moon.

When I came home I didn't see or hear Mom. I knew she was somewhere because the car was in the driveway. I was hoping to see some presents waiting for me but there were none. I went into my room and picked up the kaleidoscope. Something had happened! I still couldn't see Kip or the woman, but the images had been replaced by flowers. I turned the kaleidoscope again.

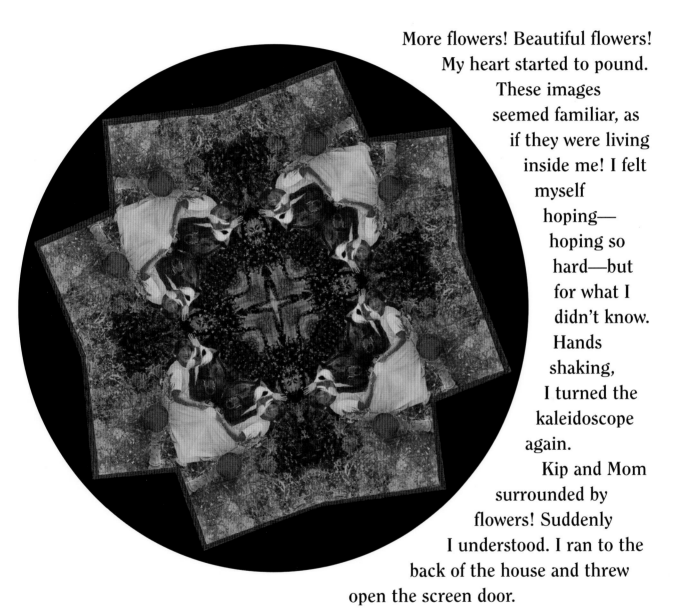

More flowers! Beautiful flowers!
My heart started to pound.
These images
seemed familiar, as
if they were living
inside me! I felt
myself
hoping—
hoping so
hard—but
for what I
didn't know.
Hands
shaking,
I turned the
kaleidoscope
again.
Kip and Mom
surrounded by
flowers! Suddenly
I understood. I ran to the
back of the house and threw
open the screen door.

Mom was sitting in a chair in her garden and beside her stood
Kip! She waved to me. "Happy Birthday, Hayley!"

"Mom, how did you get her? How long can she stay?"

"Forever. She's your birthday present from Dad and me."

I hugged Mom and Kip. "I kept looking through the kaleidoscope hoping I'd see her again. And today—just a few minutes ago—I saw her."

"Kip was in the kaleidoscope?"

"And flowers. Then you, too—here in the garden. That's how I knew you were out here. You were wearing this dress, too."

Mom shook her head in amazement.

"Don't you believe me, Mom? It's true. It's not something my eyes made up."

Mom pulled me close and gave me a hug. "I believe you, Hayley. I'm not sure I understand, but I believe you."

Mom led me through her garden and told me how she got Kip. "When you were in the hospital I saw the woman feeding Kip hay and I asked her if she owned the pony. She said she saw her just after we moved in and was shocked by how she looked. She tracked down her owner and bought Kip.

"I asked if she would consider selling the pony but she said that nobody had enough money to buy her. I thanked her and started to leave, but then she said—and I remember her words exactly—'Some things can be purchased only by the heart. Kip already belongs to your daughter.'"

"That woman had gray hair, wire glasses, and the kindest face you've ever seen, didn't she, Mom?"

"Yes, she did. How did you know that?"

"She gave me the kaleidoscope in the hospital. She taught me that sometimes what is real and what is magic are the same. And that one truly sees—"

Mom and I finished together—"with the heart."

From that day on, the kaleidoscope images remained beautiful designs, and I was happy with that. I told Mom that I wanted to thank the woman. Mom had called her several times on the phone to plan my birthday surprise. But when I dialed the number Mom gave me, a recording said that the number had been disconnected. I tried again but got the same recording. Mom said she must have moved.

That summer Dad came to stay for good and he built Kip a shed. Every day I rode her through the woods behind our house. We jumped logs, forded streams, and galloped up and down hills. I let Kip graze in meadows filled with wildflowers. We saw deer, herons, and even a fox. I did a lot of other things, too, like swimming in Walden Pond with friends. I read books and took a drawing class at a local museum. But what I liked best was being with Kip.

I never did talk again with the
woman in the kaleidoscope.
But each day when Kip and
I turned onto the trail
that would lead us to
our next adventure,
I thanked her silently.
I thanked her for the
truth and the magic
that she and Kip had
brought into my life.
Even though my eyes
couldn't see her, I was
certain she could see us.
And I saw her—and I still
can see her—with my heart.